5-MINUTE FURRY FRIENDS STORIES

DISNEY PRESS

Los Angeles • New York

CONTENTS

A Day with Papa

Thumper was terribly excited. He and his dad were spending the day together, just the two of them.

"Papa and I are going to have some great adventures in the forest," he told his sisters.

Thumper wondered what Papa had planned. Maybe they would climb a mountain . . . or explore a cave. . . .

"I thought we'd gather some greens for supper," Papa Bunny said. "Remember, eating greens is a special treat. It makes long ears—and great big feet!"

"Yes, Papa," said Thumper, his heart sinking.

Thumper and Papa got straight to work.
A little while later, Thumper wanted a nice cool drink.
"Don't dawdle," said Papa Bunny.
"I won't, Papa," replied Thumper. And off he went.

While Thumper had some water, he saw ducks splashing near a waterfall.

He wished he could join them.

But Thumper knew that Papa was waiting.

He hadn't hopped very far when he saw the frogs playing. *Ribbit, ribbit!*

That sure seemed like fun!

Then Thumper remembered Papa, hard at work.

After a few more hops, Thumper saw his friend the opossum.

"Want to climb this tree with me?" the opossum asked.

"Okay!" Thumper said, forgetting about his papa.

With a little boost from his friend, Thumper was soon exploring
the old oak tree.

The two peered into a bird's nest. *Chirp, chirp!*

They woke up a sleepy owl. *Whooooooooo!*

They got close, but not *too* close, to a buzzing beehive. *Bzzz, bzzz.*

"Well, it's time for me to go," the opossum said after a while. "My father is waiting for me."

Uh-oh! Thumper remembered his own papa.

Thumper looked down. The ground was very far away.

How would he ever get back on the ground?

As Thumper waited, a little squirrel came by. "Well, hello there, Thumper," she said. "Why don't you use your claws to get down?" But Thumper didn't have claws.

Thumper sighed. "Only one person can help me," he said.

"*Whooo?*" asked the owl.

"My papa," said Thumper sadly.

"I thought you'd never ask!" came a voice from down below. "I've been looking for you everywhere."

"Papa?" Thumper asked.

"Yes, Thumper, it's me," Papa Bunny replied. "Now take a deep breath and look down."

Thumper opened his eyes. His papa was reaching for him.

The ground looked a lot closer now. Thumper reached down, and his father pulled him tight.

"You must never be afraid to ask me for help. I am your father, and I will always be here for you," Papa Bunny said.

"I know, Papa," said Thumper.

"Well, all work and no play makes for a bored little bunny!" said
Papa. "Why don't we race back to the meadow? Then we'll explore a
hidden cave. The last one there is a slowpoke!"

That night, the bunnies ate fresh greens. Everyone agreed they were
ever so tasty.

"Did you have lots of adventures?" Tessie asked.

"Why, yes," boasted Thumper. "I even climbed a tree!"

"Oh, my," said Daisy. "Were you scared?"

"What a silly question," Trixie scoffed. "Thumper is never scared."
Thumper looked at Papa, who gave him a big wink. Thumper
grinned. He was glad he had gotten to spend the day with his papa.

Disney
Peter Pan

Nana and the Game of Hide-and-Seek

It was a rainy afternoon in London, and the Darling children stared out the window at the gray sky. Mother and Father had already left for their evening out.

"Rain again?" whined Michael, the youngest.

"It's been like this for weeks!" said John, the middle child.

"Now, boys! I know the rain is terribly dull," said Wendy, the oldest and most sensible of the three, "but let's use our imaginations. Nana, what do you think we should do?"

Nana was the Darling children's beloved dog . . . and nanny.

"Woof!" said Nana.
"But I don't wanna
play a board game.
It's boring!" said
Michael.

"Woof?" asked Nana.
"Nana, you're the
only one who thinks it's
fun to catch mice in the
house," said John.

"Woof, woof!"
suggested Nana. The
children perked up.
"Brilliant idea, Nana! We
will all play hide-and-seek,"
Wendy declared.

"I'll go first," Wendy said. "You all turn around and count to twenty. When you're finished, come and find me."

"One, two, three . . ." John and Michael said in unison.

"Woof, woof, woof . . ." said Nana.

"Twenty!" the boys shouted.

"Woof!" Nana was ready to seek. Wendy
thought she had found the perfect hiding place.

But the boys found
her easily.

"Found you!" John
said, laughing.

"Wendy, why did
you hide there?"
asked Michael.
"How silly!"

"Now it's my turn to hide," said John, already thinking of where to
go. "I'll be sure to find a better hiding place than you did, Wendy!"

"Don't be so sure of it," she said.

Nana started the next countdown. "Woof, woof, woof . . ."

With all the great hiding spots in the house, John couldn't decide which to choose.

"Should I hide here?

"Or here?

"Or how about this cupboard? Or . . ."

John spent so much time running from one hiding place to the next
that the second round of hide-and-seek turned into a game of chase!

"We got you!" Michael squealed with delight. "My turn now! I know the perfect hiding spot, and I want Nana to come with me!"

"Woof?" Nana asked.

Nana and Michael went off to hide while the other two children began to count.

Michael and Nana bounded up one flight of stairs, then another, then another. Nana had never gone above the nursery's floor, and she didn't think Michael had, either.

"The attic!" Michael said proudly, pointing to an old-looking wooden door. "They'll never find us up here. We're sure to win!"

Michael pulled open the heavy door, and Nana pranced in,
delighted to be a part of the winning plan.
Bang! The door shut behind them.

"Wow!" Michael gasped.

Michael and Nana couldn't believe their eyes. The attic contained treasures beyond their wildest dreams.

"Look at all
this amazing
stuff, Nana!"
cried Michael.

"Woof, woof!" Nana agreed.

Meanwhile, Wendy and John were looking for Michael and Nana everywhere.

They grew worried as the sun began to set and they still hadn't found them.

"Where are Wendy and John?" asked Michael. He was afraid of the dark, and his voice wobbled. "It's almost nighttime. Why haven't they come to get us yet?"

Nana began to howl. Michael did, too.

"Wendy! John! We're up here!" he shouted.

"Woof! Woof! Woof!" Nana barked as loud as she could.

"Do you hear that, John?" asked Wendy.

"I think it's Nana's bark, coming from upstairs," said John. "Let's go!"

"Oh, you poor things," Wendy said, hearing Michael's and Nana's howling from outside the attic. "John, open the door."

"I can't—it's locked!" he said.

Locked? Nana suddenly remembered
something she had seen in a box.

"Oh, Nana, you lovely old thing," said
Michael. "Of course, the keys!"

Nana slipped the keys, one by one, under
the door to Wendy and John . . .

. . . who tried each key until they found one that worked. Wendy and John flung open the door, and all four of them met in a giant hug.

"I think we won the game!" declared Michael as the others burst into laughter.

And the three Darling children cheered for their beloved Nana, who had saved the day.

Pepita and Dante to the Rescue!

In the little Mexican town of Santa Cecilia, the Rivera family was busy preparing for a big celebration called Día de los Muertos—the Day of the Dead. They would honor and remember their ancestors by making an altar called an ofrenda. It held photographs, keepsakes, and food—everything that the Rivera ancestors had loved in life.

While all the preparations for the holiday looked the same, things *sounded* a bit different this year in the Rivera home. For nearly a year, Miguel had been filling the house with music. It was easy for him now that he had his family's approval. They had always thought music had torn their family apart, but it had actually brought them together.

Miguel especially loved singing "Un Poco Loco." Whenever he played it, he would remember his amazing performance with his great-great-grandfather Héctor in the Land of the Dead.

Miguel finished singing for his mamá and his little sister, Socorro.

"Bravo, Miguel!" said Mamá. "Now, can my little músico see if Abuelita needs help in the kitchen?"

Miguel's stomach rumbled. "Sure, Mamá!" he said.

As Miguel approached the kitchen, he noticed Dante and Pepita near the door. Abuelita enjoyed having Dante around more than she once had, but she had a strict no-animal policy in the kitchen.

"Come back a little later," Miguel whispered. "Abuelita will give us tamales."

Dante wagged his tail and Pepita meowed as they left.

The kitchen was filled with the smells of scrumptious food.

"Do you need help, Abuelita?" asked Miguel.

"I'm okay, mi hijo, but eat something," Abuelita said as she continued stirring. She was making the family's favorite dishes: posole, pan de muerto, mole rojo, and much more. The food would be placed on the ofrenda as an offering for their loved ones who were no longer there.

Miguel realized something. "Abuelita, what are you making for Papá Héctor?"

Abuelita dropped her wooden spoon with a loud clatter.

"Ay, dios mío! I don't know! I didn't even know who he was until last year!"

Suddenly, Miguel realized that he needed Dante and Pepita. "I have an idea, Abuelita. Uh . . . I'll be right back."

Miguel rushed off to find Dante and Pepita. They were the only ones who could help him. His family had no idea that Dante and Pepita had a secret: they were creatures of the spirit realm who could travel between the Lands of the Living and the Dead. Miguel ran down the streets of Santa Cecilia.

He found Dante and Pepita taking a nap in the gazebo near Mariachi Plaza.

"Can you get Papá Héctor a message?" Miguel asked. He scribbled a note and gave it to Dante.

Dante wagged his tail before dashing away with Pepita.

Dante and Pepita dodged the crowds in the cemetery and ran all the way to a marigold bridge that could be seen only by visiting spirits. As soon as they reached the bridge, they magically glowed as they transformed. Pepita grew from a little alley cat into a mighty flying jaguar, while Dante sprouted a pair of wings.

"Rooooo-roo-roo-roo," mumbled Dante, trying not to drop Miguel's note. He spotted a few of the dead Riveras near Marigold Grand Central Station.

The dead Riveras looked up and saw the two spirit guides overhead.

"Look, it's Pepita!" shouted Tío Felipe.

"And Dante!" said Tía Victoria.

When Dante and Pepita landed, they gave the note to Mamá Coco, who now lived in the Land of the Dead. "It's urgent," she said. "Miguel needs to know what my papá wants for the ofrenda."

"Follow us to the plaza!" Tía Victoria told Dante and Pepita.

The plaza was filled with a giant crowd. They were gathered to hear Papá Héctor and Mamá Imelda sing.

Mamá Imelda noticed the spirit guides and stopped singing. "Qué pasa? Why are Dante and Pepita here?"

Mamá Coco handed the note to Papá Héctor. He was touched that Miguel was concerned about his first Día de los Muertos. After he wrote down his favorite dish, he gave it back to Dante.

The dead Riveras waved goodbye as Dante and Pepita soared into the sky. Pepita swooped toward the Land of the Living. Dante veered slightly off course, greeting other spirit creatures nearby. But Pepita knew they were running out of time. She grabbed Dante with her talons and placed him on her back for safekeeping.

"Rooooo-roo-roo-roo!" Dante crooned as they flew over the Marigold Bridge.

Dante and Pepita transformed back into a dog and cat when they returned to Santa Cecilia. They dashed toward the Rivera house.

Miguel gave them a big hug when they arrived. "Thank you, Dante and Pepita! You saved the day!"

Miguel could not reveal Dante's and Pepita's secret identities. Instead, he told Abuelita that he found the note in one of Mamá Coco's journals. She took the paper from Miguel and kissed his head. "Gracias, Miguelito! I have just enough time to make this dish before the festivities begin."

Later that night, Papá Héctor, Mamá Imelda, Mamá Coco, and the rest of the Rivera ancestors crossed over the Marigold Bridge.

They walked through the cemetery and followed the path of marigolds that their family had left for them.

When the dead Riveras arrived at the house, they admired the ofrenda that the family had worked so hard to put together.

The whole Rivera family, both the living and dead, enjoyed
the celebration together. Even Dante and Pepita joined in on the
festivities. Miguel strummed his guitar as Dante and Pepita enjoyed
their well-deserved tamales.

The Surprise Party

Early one morning, Thomas O'Malley yawned, stretched . . . and found three little kittens jumping on his bed. Marie, Berlioz, and Toulouse began singing cheerily while Duchess presented O'Malley with a dish of cream.

"Happy birthday!" the cats sang out.

"Well, gee, that's the best birthday present I ever got!" O'Malley
exclaimed. "Thanks a bunch!" Turning to the kittens, he said, "I don't
suppose anyone wants to help me eat my breakfast?"

"Oh, thank you, Mr. O'Malley!" the kittens replied as they began
lapping the cream.

When they had finished eating, O'Malley said, "Say, I was hoping to spend some time with Scat Cat and the band—"

"Well, Thomas," Duchess quickly interrupted. "We actually have quite a big day planned for your birthday. Perhaps you can meet with them later."

"Really? Plans for *my* birthday?" O'Malley said.

"Now, children," Duchess began, "who wants to give Thomas his birthday present first?"

"I do, I do!" Toulouse replied. "Follow me, Mr. O'Malley!"

"Yeah," said Berlioz. "Follow him!"

As soon as O'Malley's back was turned, Duchess whispered to Berlioz and Marie: "Come, children! Let's get on with our plans for Thomas's surprise party!"

Toulouse led O'Malley into the sunroom.

"Today I'm gonna paint your portrait. Face this way, please, and don't move!"

Toulouse began squirting paint from various tubes.

O'Malley was so busy watching Toulouse that he didn't see what was happening behind him.

A little while later, Toulouse presented his painting to O'Malley.

"That's real swell, Toulouse," O'Malley said. "I don't suppose you could teach me how to do that."

"Sure!" Toulouse replied. "I can teach ya!" He smothered a smile. The birthday surprise plans were right on track!

Toulouse showed O'Malley how to mix paints to
get different colors. Then they outlined a picture.
They painted and painted and painted.

Suddenly, Marie and Berlioz walked into the room.

"Our turn, our turn!" Marie said to O'Malley. "Would you like to hear some scales and arpeggios?" Meanwhile, Toulouse quietly backed out of the room to help with the rest of the birthday preparations.

"We planned a special birthday song just for you!" Berlioz said.

"Wanna hear it?"

"Well, sure I do!" O'Malley said.

Berlioz and Marie made sure O'Malley was looking at them—not outside, where the others were setting up the surprise party.

Berlioz stretched along the keyboard and played their new song while Marie began to sing. O'Malley was loving the tempo and couldn't believe they had written him his very own tune. He found himself tapping and singing along, just as Berlioz and Marie had planned.

"Thank you for the best birthday song I've ever heard!" O'Malley said when they had finished.

As early evening approached, O'Malley was getting ready to find Scat Cat and the band when Duchess asked if she could take him on a birthday stroll.

They wandered all around Madame's courtyard. When they reached the end of the garden, Duchess pulled a wrapped gift from behind a rosebush.

"Happy birthday, dear Thomas," she said.

"A bow tie! Thanks, Duchess," he said. "Between you and those kittens, this has been a terrific birthday!"

"It's not over yet, you know," Duchess told him. "We do have one last surprise for you."

Duchess led O'Malley into the dining room.

"I hope everything is to your liking," Madame said to O'Malley.

Toulouse, Berlioz, and Marie were there with Roquefort, too.

"Happy birthday!" they all called out.

They had prepared all his favorite foods. "I'm stuffed," O'Malley said after enjoying the treats. "Say, what a terrific birthday! And the best part has been sharing it with all of you."

It was starting to get dark outside, and O'Malley turned to the kittens. "I think it's almost time for bed, little ones," he said.

"Before we go to bed, can we go look at the stars?" Marie asked.

"Well, sure, I don't see why not," O'Malley replied.

"Oh, yes," Duchess added as they all headed outside. "That's a wonderful idea. And Thomas! I have to confess . . . I told you a little white lie. The dinner was your second-to-last birthday surprise. . . ."

"Surprise!" yelled Duchess and the kittens.

"Surprise!" hollered Scat Cat and the band.

"Wow!" O'Malley exclaimed. Turning to Duchess and the kittens, he asked, "How did you pull this off? You were with me all day!"

Marie giggled. "Well, sometimes some of us were with you . . ."

"While others of us were preparing," Duchess concluded.

It was a fantastic celebration, and
everyone had a wonderful time.

Berlioz, Toulouse, and Marie even
got to stay up late to enjoy the fun.

When the night finally ended, O'Malley turned to Duchess and the kittens. "Thanks for the best birthday I ever had! It's over now, right?" he said, laughing.

Duchess smiled at him. "Your birthday is over, but I think we'll keep on celebrating you being in our lives for a long time yet. Right, children?"

"Yes," Toulouse whispered, yawning. "Happy birthday to you, Abraham DeLacey Giuseppe Casey Thomas O'Malley!"

A Surprise for Pluto

One sunny morning, Mickey Mouse looked out the window. "What a beautiful day!" he exclaimed. "This is perfect building weather."

His nephews, Morty and Ferdie, joined him. "What are you going to build, Uncle Mickey?" asked Morty.

Mickey's eyes twinkled. "Oh, I don't know," he said. "Maybe . . . a tree house!"

The boys jumped up and down. "A tree house?" Ferdie said.

"Can we help?" Morty asked.

"You would be great helpers," Mickey replied. "But there will be lots of tools in the yard. It might not be very safe. Why don't you take Pluto to the park instead?"

"Sure, Uncle Mickey!" the boys replied.

With Morty, Ferdie, and Pluto gone, Mickey called his friends. He told them all about the tree house and asked if they would like to help. Soon Minnie, Donald, Daisy, and Goofy arrived in Mickey's yard.

"Building a tree house is a big job," Mickey said. "Maybe we should split up the work."

"Great idea, Mickey," Goofy said.

"Why don't you saw the boards, Goofy?" Mickey said. "Then Donald and I can hammer them together."

Minnie showed Mickey a special drawing she had made.

"Good thinking, Minnie!" Mickey said. "That will be one of the most important jobs of all."

Goofy dumped out his toolbox in a corner of the yard. The tools made a big crash—and a big mess! Goofy found what he was looking for and began sawing the boards.

After a few minutes, Minnie walked up to him. "Sorry to bother you, Goofy," she began. "I was wondering if you would cut some boards for me, too."

"Sure!" Goofy said with a grin. "Just tell me what you need."

Over by the big tree, Donald and Mickey worked together to make a rope ladder. When they were finished, Mickey attached the ladder to the thickest branch. He gave the ladder a strong tug. It didn't budge.

"That should do it," Mickey said. "Once we finish building, we can use this ladder to climb into the tree house."

Just then, Goofy brought them a stack of boards. "Here you go!" he said. "I still have to saw the boards for the roof, but you can use these for the floor and the walls."

"Thanks, Goofy!" Mickey said.

Mickey and Donald climbed into the tree, pulling the boards behind them. The sounds of their hammers echoed through the backyard as the friends started building.

Across the yard, Minnie pulled her hammer out of her tool belt. As she picked up the first board, she realized that she had forgotten something very important.

Minnie hurried over to the big tree. "Do you have any extra nails?" she called up. "I left all of mine at home!"

"I have some," Donald said. He fished a box of nails out of his tool belt and gave them to Minnie.

On the way back to her project, Minnie stopped to see how Daisy was doing.

"Wow, Daisy," Minnie said. "You mixed up a lot of paint!"

Daisy giggled. "I might have mixed a little *too* much," she said. "Do you need any paint for your project?"

"Thanks, Daisy," Minnie said. "That would be great!"

Soon everyone was hard at work.

Buzz-buzz-buzz went the saw.

Bang-bang-bang went the hammers.

Swish-swish-swish went the paintbrushes.

Mickey's backyard was a very busy place!

Later that day, Morty, Ferdie, and Pluto came home from the park. Morty and Ferdie couldn't believe their eyes. "Wow!" the boys cried.

"This is the best tree house ever!" added Ferdie as they scrambled up the rope ladder.

Beneath them, Pluto whined. He couldn't climb the ladder like the others.

Mickey understood right away. "Don't worry, Pluto!" he called. "Come around to the other side of the tree."

Pluto trotted around the tree and found something that made his tail wag: a set of stairs that was just his size!

"Minnie made them for you," Mickey explained. "Now come on up and join the fun!"

Pluto ran up the stairs. It really *was* the best tree house ever!

DISNEY

THE

LION KING

A Prince's Day

It was early morning at Pride Rock. Simba and Nala couldn't wait to go out and play. "Let's go down to the river!" Nala shouted.

"Shhh," Simba whispered. "We have to be quiet or Zazu will hear us."

But it was too late. Zazu had been on the lookout for the young prince.

"Ahh! There you are, Simba," Zazu said, landing in front of Simba. "Come along. We have a busy day of training ahead of us."

"But Nala and I were about to go down to the river!" Simba complained.

"Nonsense," Zazu said. "As a prince you have certain responsibilities, young sire. And we can't keep them waiting."

"Bye, Simba!" Nala said. "Have fun at prince school! Maybe we can go to the river tomorrow."

"Not if Zazu has anything to say about it," Simba grumbled, watching as Nala bounded away.

Zazu led Simba down to the watering hole, where the animals of the Pride Lands were taking turns drinking water.

"Part of a ruler's responsibilities is solving disputes between his subjects. A perfect example is the watering hole! Each animal needs to have a turn to drink," Zazu explained. "See that herd of antelopes? They have been here too long. It's the rhinos' turn!

"You! You there!" the bird said, yelling at the antelopes.

Simba listened for what felt like hours as Zazu talked on and on to the antelopes.

Finally, the lion cub saw a chance to escape. A herd of giraffes was leaving the watering hole. If he could sneak out with them, he might still have time to play with Nala!

Just when Simba thought he had gotten away, Zazu landed in front of him.

"And where do you think you're going?" Zazu demanded.

"Come on, Zazu. We've been at the watering hole for hours. Can't I go play with Nala?" Simba asked.

But Zazu refused to let him go. "A prince's job is never done!" he insisted. "Onward to our next stop!"

Zazu led Simba back to Pride Rock, where Mufasa was listening to his subjects' concerns.

"A king must listen to all the other animals," Zazu explained. "You can learn a lot from your father."

Simba tried to pay attention. He listened as Mufasa advised the
elephants to find new grazing grounds. He listened as the zebras
worried about the upcoming rainy season.

But soon the lion cub was just as bored as he had been at the
watering hole. He started to fall asleep.

"Young sire!" Zazu yelled, angrily pecking Simba awake. "Were you paying any attention at all?"

Simba yawned, shaking himself awake. He looked around. The other animals were gone. Mufasa must have finished for the day.

"Um, I heard some of it?" Simba replied.

Frustrated, Zazu flew up in the air. "Come along, Simba. We aren't finished yet," Zazu said.

Simba slowly followed as the bird led him away from Pride Rock. Soon they were walking past the river where Simba and Nala had planned to play that day. Simba looked for his friend, but he didn't see her.

Suddenly, Simba heard a yell. "Did you hear that, Zazu?" he asked.

"Hear what, Simba?" Zazu said.

There was another yell. "That!" Simba said, running toward the river. Zazu flew after him.

It was Nala. She had fallen into the fast-moving river and couldn't get out!

"Hurry, go get my father!" Simba ordered Zazu.

The bird flew away in search of Mufasa, but Simba knew there wasn't time to wait. Nala needed him now!

Simba looked everywhere for a way to get to his best friend. Finally, he saw a long tree branch on the shore of the river.

"Nala! Grab on!" Simba yelled. He grabbed the tree branch in his mouth and moved it over the river. Nala reached out and grabbed the branch just in time!

Simba pulled the branch back and dragged Nala out of the river. She was safe!

"Simba? Simba!" Mufasa called, running to the river.

"Here, Dad!" Simba said, panting. "It's okay! I got Nala!"

Relieved, Mufasa and Zazu gathered the cubs and started back to Pride Rock.

"Zazu, Nala, can you give me a moment with Simba?" Mufasa asked. Simba was worried. Was Mufasa angry at him for not paying attention to Zazu?

"Zazu told me about your day. I know that you want to play with your friend, but Zazu was trying to teach you important lessons about what it means to be king," Mufasa said.

"What did you learn at the watering hole?" Mufasa asked.

"That the rhinos follow the antelopes?" Simba replied.

Mufasa laughed. "No, that you have to be fair as a ruler and make sure all your subjects are treated equally," he said. "And Zazu brought you to Pride Rock to show you that a leader must be wise as well. But the last lesson, you taught yourself."

"I did?" Simba said.

"Yes, my son. You rescued Nala and showed that a ruler must be brave. I am very proud of you, Simba."

Simba smiled up at his father.

"Now," Mufasa said, "I think there may just be enough time for you and Nala to play before dinner."

Simba smiled and bounded off to find Nala.

"He'll make a good king someday, sire," Zazu said, landing on Mufasa's shoulder.

Mufasa smiled. "Yes, he will."

Watch Dug

Dug bounded over some rocks, scrambled up a hill, and crossed a little stream. The golden retriever was looking for a spot to camp for the night.

Following him were his friends Carl Fredricksen and Russell. Dug had met them in South America when Carl and Russell were on an adventure. Dug wanted to find the best camping spot ever—just for them!

Around his neck, Dug wore a high-tech collar that helped him speak to humans. "Find the spot. Find the spot," he chanted aloud.

Suddenly, Dug saw a good place. "POINT!" he shouted. He froze and pointed toward a clearing up ahead. It had trees on three sides and a beautiful view across a valley.

Russell and Carl looked around.

"I like it!" Russell said.

Carl put down a picnic basket that held their dinner and breakfast for the next day. Next to it he placed a jug of lemonade. "Okay, Russell, let's set up those tents of yours," he said.

The day had been full of new
sights and sounds. Carl, Russell, and Dug
had hiked along a trail and climbed to a beautiful overlook.
But now the day was over, and the sun was setting.

Carl and Russell put up the tents and unrolled their
sleeping bags. They cooked dinner over the campfire, and
afterward they roasted marshmallows.

But Russell's yawns were getting bigger. It was bedtime. His
eyes half closed, Russell started to walk toward his tent.

"Hey, look at this!" he suddenly shouted.

Carl and Dug went to Russell. On the ground just past the campfire was a trail of paw prints. They all stared. Dug sniffed the tracks.

"What kind of animal made these?" Carl asked.

"A bear!" Russell shouted.

"No." Carl frowned. "They're too small."

"I'll check my *Wilderness Explorers' Handbook*," said Russell.

But Carl shook his head. "Bedtime," he instructed.

"I will keep watch all night!" Dug exclaimed. "I will find out. Do not worry. I will not fall asleep!"

"Good night, Dug," Russell said. He gave the dog a big hug.

He and Carl went into their tents and zipped up the flaps.

Dug was proud to have such an important job. He was going to be a super watchdog! Dug sat outside the tents, as still as a statue. His tail wanted to wag, but Dug wouldn't let it.

But wait! What was that by the oak tree? A squirrel?

Dug charged toward the tree—and tripped over a rope on Russell's tent. Part of the tent collapsed!

Dug hung his head. He hadn't meant for that to happen. He waited for Russell to come out. Then he heard a snore. Russell was still sleeping!

Dug slunk back to his watching spot. He had made one mistake. But that could happen to any watchdog.

The moon rose higher into the sky. Dug wanted to howl at the moon, but that would wake up Carl and Russell. So he buried his nose under his paw.

Then Dug got an itch on his back. He rolled over to scratch it.

At that moment, a bat swooped down over the clearing! Dug jumped up in surprise. He accidentally knocked over the jug of lemonade behind him, and it spilled all over the ground.

Embarrassed, Dug went to stand guard near Carl's tent. It wasn't as messy over there.

Dug watched as the moon traveled across the night sky. All was quiet.

Rustle, rustle, rustle. What was that noise? There, by the picnic basket! *Rustle, rustle. Crack!*

Dug sneaked across the clearing, keeping low to the ground. He spotted fresh paw prints in the dirt. Then he saw a shadow near a tree. Something was prowling. Now it was rummaging.

"Woof, woof, woof!" Dug barked.

The intruder turned toward him. It had a black mask and a striped tail. It was a raccoon, and it was trying to get the food in the picnic basket!

Not on Dug's watch!

"Move away from the basket!" he said. "That is our breakfast. You cannot eat it!"

The raccoon grabbed a string of sausages in its teeth. Dug took the other end. He tugged. The raccoon tugged. Dug tugged harder. The raccoon hissed. Dug growled.

Finally, the raccoon let go. Dug had won!

Defeated, the raccoon scampered away.

Dug triumphantly carried the sausages back to the picnic basket. They were a little roughed up—and dirty. A couple of leaves were stuck to the slobbery spots.

But he was sure Carl and Russell wouldn't mind.

Dug was proud of himself. He had spotted the intruder
in the dark and scared it away. He had even saved
breakfast. He felt like a top watchdog.

Soon the sky began to lighten, and the stars started to fade. Dug was very sleepy. His eyes felt *soooo* heavy. His paws felt *soooo* heavy. His ears and nose and tail felt *soooo* heavy, too. But he couldn't give up standing guard now: it was almost morning. Dug put his head down on his paws. He would rest for just a minute and then go back to keeping watch.

Resting his head felt nice. Maybe he should rest his eyes for a minute, too. It was getting harder and harder to keep them open.

Dug closed his eyes. He wasn't going to sleep, though. He was going to stay up all night to make sure Carl and Russell were safe. Nothing was going to bother them, not as long as . . .

Honk-shoooo . . . Honk-shooo . . .

Dug fell asleep.

A few minutes later, Carl came out of his tent. He no longer slept as long as he used to.

Carl looked around the clearing. He noticed Russell's tent and heard the boy still snoring. He saw the dirty sausages sticking out of the picnic basket and the jug of lemonade on its side.

Carl sat next to Dug. Dug opened one eye. "I found him. I found the creature that made the paw prints," he said.

"Yes, I heard you," Carl said. He gave Dug a pat on the head. "Good dog. Good Dug."

"Is it breakfast time yet?" Russell suddenly called from inside his tent.

"No, go back to sleep!" Carl replied. After a moment, Russell's snoring continued.

Then, together, Dug and Carl watched the sun rise over the misty valley.

Fire Pup of the Day

One morning at the farm, Rolly watched the start of a new day from his favorite sunny spot.

His father, Pongo, accompanied Roger to milk the cows. His mother, Perdita, watched Anita collect eggs. Their housekeeper, Nanny, picked fresh apples from the tree.

Fresh apples! That could mean only one thing: Nanny planned to bake an apple pie that afternoon.

Rolly yipped with glee. He ran inside to tell the others.

He found his siblings watching *The Thunderbolt Adventure Hour* on TV. The canine hero was putting out a fire. "Go, Thunderbolt, go!" Penny yelled.

"Penny! Patch!" Rolly shouted. "I have good news!" But his siblings weren't listening.

"One day, I'll be a fire hero just like Thunderbolt!" Patch exclaimed.

"Me too!" Penny replied.

"Oh, yeah?" Patch said. "You think you're fast enough?"

"Sure am!" Penny yelled. "Race ya!"

Rolly sighed as his siblings sprinted toward the front door—just as Roger, Anita, and Nanny came inside.

"Whoa there, Patch," Roger cried as milk spilled on the pup.

"Careful, Penny!" Anita exclaimed as an egg splattered near their feet.

"Oh, boy," Nanny added. "Our house has gone to the dogs!"

Pongo and Perdita arrived home next.

"Settle down, children," Pongo said. "You must be more careful."

"But, Dad," Penny pleaded, "we're practicing to become fire pups."

"I have an idea," Perdita replied. "Let's go to the barn."

In the barn, Perdita and Pongo set up a series of challenges.

"Now, puppies," Perdita said, "here are three fire safety training exercises. Let's see if any of you are ready to become junior fire pups."

The puppies barked their approval.

"Firefighters must keep their hoses neat," Perdita explained. "Let's see how quickly you can coil a garden hose."

Patch and Penny ran in perfect circles with their hoses.

Rolly tried his best, but when he finished, he had
tangled himself into one giant knot.

"Next, firefighters use ladders to rescue people," Perdita said.

"Let's see who can climb the ladder the fastest."

The puppies hurried up the ladder. But Rolly was afraid of heights. He became dizzy and fell, bumping each rung on the way down.

Clunk, clunk, clunk!

Perdita rushed to him. "Oh, no, Rolly! Are you hurt?"

"I'm fine," Rolly said. He was just disappointed.

The final challenge was a race to the fire hydrant at the edge of the farm.

"What's the use?" Rolly said. "I can't keep up."

"You're doing wonderfully," Perdita told him. "Don't give up."

Rolly shrugged as he went to the starting line.

"Ready . . . set . . . *go!*" Pongo yelled.

Rolly quickly fell behind. Disheartened, he slowed down to catch his breath. But he noticed something unusual. He'd expected to smell Nanny's delicious apple pie, but instead he smelled smoke.

Rolly forgot about the race and scuttled into the kitchen.

Sure enough, smoke rose from the oven. The pie was burning.

Rolly thought about what Thunderbolt would do. He gathered all his might and barked as loud as he could.

Soon Anita, Roger, and Nanny ran in.

"Oh, my!" Nanny exclaimed, turning off the oven. "I forgot about my pie!"

To help, Anita and Roger opened the window and the door. Pongo, Perdita, Penny, and Patch arrived just as the smoke cleared.

"Good thing you smelled the smoke, Rolly," Roger said.

"Otherwise, there could have been a real fire!"

"You're a hero!" Anita exclaimed.

"Say," said Roger, "why don't we stop by the firehouse so we can tell the team about our very own rescue pup?"

Before they left, Nanny gave the puppies some pie scraps.

"I guess it's not always important to be the fastest," Patch admitted.

"Or the strongest," Penny added.

"But we can all be brave and save the day!" Rolly said with his mouth full.

The trip to the firehouse was everything Rolly had dreamed it
would be!

He saw fire trucks and met real firefighters.

"Great work today," the captain said as he placed a fire helmet on
Rolly's head. "You must have a real nose for safety."

Rolly smiled. *I could get used to being a hero*, he thought.

Winnie the Pooh

The Forgiving Friend

It was a beautiful sunny day. Pooh went to visit his friend Rabbit. Rabbit was hard at work in his garden. Everything he had planted was ready to pick!

Pooh thought it would be good if their friends came to help. "Brilliant idea, Pooh," said Rabbit. "Do hurry and bring everyone here. We've got a big job ahead of us."

Pooh gathered his other friends and asked them to help Rabbit. They all agreed that they would meet at the garden later, after Piglet and Pooh went to check on a sick Roo.

At Kanga's house, Roo was very happy to see his good friends.

"How are you feeling today, Roo?" asked Piglet.

"I'd feel better if I had some of Mama's vegetable soup," said Roo. "But we don't have any vegetables, so she can't make it."

Piglet told Pooh he had an idea and he would be right back. Piglet went straight to Rabbit's house to ask for some vegetables. But when he got there, he could not find Rabbit or any of his other friends.

"I don't think Rabbit would mind if I took these for Roo," Piglet said, eyeing the vegetables in the garden.

Piglet hurried back to Kanga's house and saw that Pooh had already left.

"Why don't you stay and have some vegetable soup with us, Piglet?" asked Kanga. "I know it would cheer Roo up enormously!"

Later, when the rest of the friends made their way to Rabbit's garden, they saw that the vegetables had already been picked.

"This calls for a little investiggerating," said Tigger. "And I intend to get to the bottomous of the case of the disappearing vegeterribles!"

First Tigger approached Rabbit. "Now, Long Ears," he began, "where were you on the morning of—"

"Don't be ridiculous," said Rabbit. "Why would I take my own vegetables? Go bother someone else, Tigger. I've got work to do!"

So Tigger headed off through the wood. He questioned all his friends about the vegetables, but he learned nothing.

Just then, Tigger realized that he hadn't been to visit Roo. "I gotta go see my little buddy!"

When Tigger got to Roo's house, he saw that Kanga had cooked up a storm! "Did all these vegetables come from your garden?" he asked.

"Why, no, Tigger," said Kanga. "Piglet was kind enough to bring them."

"And where do you suppose he got them?" asked Tigger suspiciously.

"From Rabbit's garden, of course," she replied.

Aha! The case of the mysterious disappearing
"vegeterribles" was solved.

"I knew it all along!" cried Tigger. "I've got to go tell
ol' Long Ears! Be back in a jifferoo, little buddy!"

Tigger bounded fast and furiously to Rabbit's house. When he told him that the mystery had been solved, Rabbit was not pleased.

"Piglet should have asked before taking my vegetables," said Rabbit. "And I plan to tell him so!"

Tigger and Rabbit found Piglet at Pooh's house. Rabbit was ready to give Piglet a piece of his mind. But then he saw Piglet approaching him with a basket.

"I wanted to ask you first, Rabbit," Piglet began, "but you weren't home. I didn't think you'd mind, since the vegetables were for Roo. Here, take these haycorn muffins as an 'I'm sorry' gift."

Rabbit softened after listening to Piglet. "Never mind, Piglet. I forgive you."

Then he looked at Piglet's basket. "Why don't we take your muffins and the last of my vegetables over to Kanga and Roo right now?"

At Roo's house, Rabbit and Piglet presented their gifts. Everyone was happy to see Roo was feeling better.

"I hope you're planning to stay for dinner," said Kanga.

"This forgiveness business looks pretty tasty," said Tigger.

"Let's eat!" said Pooh.

Barking up the Right Tree

"What a day!" Tramp said, gazing out the window into the garden. "C'mon! What are we waitin' for? Let's go outside and do something fun!" he called to Lady.

Lady jumped up from her cozy cushion and happily padded toward the doggy door. "Why don't we play hide-and-seek?" she suggested.

"That's a swell idea," said Tramp. "Last one outside is it!"

A few minutes later, Tramp was busy counting. "Seven . . . eight . . . nine . . . ten! Ready or not, here I come!" he said.

Tramp opened his eyes and quickly scanned the garden. He looked right. He looked left. He looked up *and* down. Finally, he saw them: two dainty pale-brown paws peeking out from beneath the flowers!

"Gotcha!" Tramp said, playfully pouncing paws-first into the flowers. "Me-*ow*!"

"Hey!" Tramp cried. The next thing he knew, a blur of soft brown-and-white fur was hurtling past him. Startled, he fell into a rosebush.

"What was *that*?" Lady gasped, jumping out from behind the doghouse, where she had been hiding.

Tramp pointed to the thick trunk of the shady old elm tree. A fluffy brown-and-white kitten was racing straight up to the nearest branch.

"Oh, poor thing," Lady cooed. "You must have scared her, Tramp."

"Scared *her*?" Tramp frowned, shaking the thorns out of his tail. "More like she scared *me*!"

"Oh, Tramp," said Lady. "Don't tell me a little kitten scared you. It's all right," she called up to the kitten. "Tramp was only playing. We're sorry if you're frightened. Trust me, we'd never hurt you. It's perfectly safe to come back down."

The kitten peered down from her branch, looking scared.

"Oh, won't you please come down?" Lady urged her.

But the kitten didn't move.

"Aw, shucks. Lemme talk to her," said Tramp, stretching up to rest his front paws against the tree. "Here, kitty," he called. "C'mon down. I'm sorry. I know I can seem a little, uh, big and scary, but really, we were just playing a game of hide-and-seek."

At last, the kitten moved, but only to tiptoe farther along the branch.

"Looks like she's happy up there," Tramp said, shrugging.

"Or stuck!" Lady said. "Oh, Tramp, we have to help her down!"

Tramp didn't have much interest in helping the kitten out of the tree, but he would do anything for Lady. And Lady had a plan—a plan that seemed like it just might work *if* he helped her.

"You stand here, next to the tree, and let me climb on your back," Lady told Tramp. "Then, maybe, if I stretch as far as I can, I can reach that kitten and help her down."

As it so happened, at that very moment, Jock was strolling by the garden and decided to drop in.

"Well, I must say! This is a grand sight!" he exclaimed as he spotted Tramp and Lady. "You certainly don't see somethin' like this every day, now, do you? Would this be a new trick Darling and Jim Dear taught you?"

"Oh, no. It's no trick," Lady told Jock. She explained that she and Tramp were trying to help the kitten down from the tree. "Unfortunately, I can't get high enough," Lady said.

"Aye, I can see that, lass," Jock replied.

"Maybe if you climbed up and stood on me . . ." Lady began.

"Say no more!" Jock told her. "As ever, my lady, I am at your service!"

A few minutes later, Trusty wandered over from his front porch. "Well, I do declare," he said, even more surprised than Jock had been. "Miss Lady, what in the world are you and Jock doing up *there*?"

Lady explained the situation. "I see, I see," Trusty said.

"Unfortunately," sighed Lady, "we still can't reach the kitten. But maybe if *you* helped us, Trusty . . ."

"Why, Miss Lady," replied Trusty, "what kind of gentleman would I be if I didn't oblige such a request?"

"Was that a yes or a no?" Tramp asked. "I can't tell."

"I believe that would be an aye," said Jock.

"Alrighty, then. Let's do this thing!" Tramp said.

Carefully, everyone
climbed down. Then Tramp
climbed onto Trusty's back,
and Lady and Jock climbed
back into place.

"Can you reach the
branch now, Jock?" Lady
called up to him.

"Aye!" said Jock,
wagging his tail.

"Awoo!" howled Trusty,
so happy that he didn't
notice the butterfly landing
on his nose . . . until
it was too late.

Suddenly, Trusty's howl turned into a howling sneeze!

Before the dogs knew it, their hard-fought tower had collapsed into a furry twelve-legged pile.

Twelve legs? Lady counted again. *Shouldn't there be sixteen legs?* she thought. "Where's Jock?" she asked.

"Up here, lassie!"

Lady looked up, along with Tramp and Trusty, to see Jock dangling by his front paws from the branch.

"I don't suppose you could get back up here in a hurry," Jock called down as calmly as he could. "I'm having a wee bit of trouble holding on."

Quickly, the dogs re-formed their tower. At the bottom, Trusty
kept an eye out for any butterflies, determined to hold his ground this
time. At the top, Jock regained his footing on Lady's shoulders.

"Here, kitty, kitty . . ." he said gently. "Here—"

"Is something wrong?" Lady asked when Jock suddenly stopped.

"Aye," Jock answered, looking up and down the branch. "There is
one wee problem, I'm afraid."

The kitten was not on the branch anymore. In fact, the kitten wasn't even in the tree!

"Why, I do declare!" Trusty exclaimed, looking down. "If that li'l ol' kitten ain't a-rubbin' my back leg!"

"Aye, so she is!" Jock said.

"You've gotta be kidding me," Tramp groaned.

"I just love happy endings, don't you?" Lady asked when everyone was back on the ground.

Jock and Trusty agreed.

"Yeah, they're okay, I guess," Tramp said as the kitten took a turn around his leg. "But you know what I like even better?"

"What?" Lady asked.

"Playing hide-and-seek! Hey, kitten! You're it!"

Disney DUMBO

Timothy's Big Day

Timothy Q. Mouse looked over the edge of Dumbo's hat and grinned. Below him, the crowd cheered for the flying elephant.

Timothy loved the circus. He loved the noise and the lights and the looks on the audience's faces when they saw something amazing. There was no place in the world he would rather be.

Later that night, Timothy watched the crew pack up the circus. It was time to move on to a new town. Timothy heard the Ringmaster shout, "Mail call!" A tiny envelope, unnoticed by the Ringmaster, fell out of his pile and fluttered to the floor.

Timothy scurried over to it. He never got mail, but when he turned the envelope over, he gasped. It was for him!

Timothy hurried to Dumbo's stall.

"Oh, boy! Look at this, will ya?" Timothy shouted, waving around the letter. "My parents are coming to see you perform, Dumbo. They've never liked the circus, but seeing our show will change that! After all, who wouldn't love a flying elephant?"

As the circus traveled to the next town, Timothy grew more and more excited about seeing his parents.

But Timothy was nervous, too. What if his parents didn't think he'd done a good job with Dumbo after all? He wanted them to be proud of him. And that meant he had to show them how great circus life was.

The next morning, the circus train pulled into the station. After he'd been away so long, Timothy felt strange being home again.

He wondered if he would see his family in the crowd. But there were too many people. If the mice had come, there was no way he'd be able to find them.

Finally, the animals arrived at the circus site. Timothy watched as the circus hands got to work setting up the big top. No matter how many times he saw it, watching the tent go up never got any less exciting.

"Just wait until my family gets a load of this," Timothy said to Dumbo. "The lights. The noise. And you, Dumbo. I can't wait for them to see your act."

But at that moment, Dumbo let out a great big sneeze.

Dumbo sneezed again. And again.

"Oh, no," the Ringmaster said, hurrying over to look at the little elephant. "This is no good. You can't go on with a cold, and we can't go on without you."

The Ringmaster turned to the circus hands. "Sorry, lads. This fella needs his rest. Tonight's show will have to wait."

Timothy looked at Dumbo. The Ringmaster was right: the little elephant did not look good at all.

"It's my job to take care of you, Dumbo," Timothy said with determination. "Let's find you somewhere comfortable to lie down."

Timothy led Dumbo to a cozy pile of hay and went to get a steaming bowl of peanut soup.

Timothy started to give
Dumbo a warm bath, but
Dumbo sneezed again.

Next the mouse found the
warmest blanket he could and
draped it over Dumbo. But it
was no use. The elephant just
kept sneezing.

"Well, the least I can do is make sure you get some peace and quiet so you can rest," Timothy said, heading outside the tent to stand guard.

He felt bad for Dumbo. It was no fun to be sick. But he felt bad for himself, too. This had been his chance to make his parents proud of him.

Timothy was still feeling sorry for
himself a few hours later when he heard a
familiar voice.

"Timothy, dear. We have been looking
for you everywhere!"

Timothy turned to see his mother, his father, and his brothers and
sisters standing in front of him.

"Mother. Father. You're here." The little mouse hung his head. "I'm
afraid Dumbo has a cold. He can't go on tonight. I'm sorry you wasted
your time coming."

"Wasted our time?" Timothy's father asked. "We came to the circus to see *you*. We're not big-city travelers, but we're certainly not going to miss a chance to see our son!"

"You don't think I made a mistake joining the circus?" Timothy asked.

"There's no such thing as a mistake as long as you're doing what you love," his mother said.

At that moment, the flaps to Dumbo's tent rustled, and the little elephant stepped through, looking like he felt much better. Something Timothy had done must have helped after all.

"Dumbo, old pal," Timothy said, "may I introduce you to my family?"

Dumbo was very pleased to meet them.

"If you'll excuse me," Timothy said to everyone, "I'd better let the Ringmaster know that Dumbo is feeling better. But . . . wait here, you two. I have something I'd like to show you."

That night, as Dumbo prepared to take to the air, Timothy
climbed into his usual spot on the elephant's hat. But this time, he
wasn't alone. Beside him were his parents.

"Hold on tight!" Timothy called.

With a great flapping of his ears, Dumbo lifted
off the ground and soared over the circus crowd.
Cheers filled the room at the sight of the flying
elephant in action.

From their perch on Dumbo's hat, Timothy's parents looked at the crowd below them.

"You know, Son," Timothy's father said, "all those happy faces are pretty special. Maybe I'm starting to understand this circus thing after all."

Timothy's mother nodded and gave her son a hug.

"Now, tell me," she said, "can this elephant go any faster?"

Stitch's Day at School

Lilo and Stitch were excited. It was Pet Day at school. All the kids were bringing their pets to class.

"Hurry up, Lilo!"
Nani, Lilo's older sister,
called. "You'll be late
for school!"

Nani looked at Stitch. "We're going to be on our best behavior today, right?"

Stitch nodded. He was very excited to go to Lilo's school.

At school, there were all different kinds of pets. Some were big and fluffy. Some were small and scaly. Some even looked like their owners!

The class also had a
pet of its own, a frog named
Mr. Phibbs. But none of the animals
looked like Stitch.

After each presentation, Lilo got more and more excited. She couldn't wait for her turn. Stitch was curious about all the different creatures.

But when he tried to get a closer look at the class pet . . . . . . Mr. Phibbs jumped out of his habitat and disappeared through the door.

Stitch chased Mr. Phibbs. The frog hopped down the hall and into another classroom.

In that classroom, students wore goggles and aprons as they worked on experiments.

It reminded Stitch of Jumba's lab. Stitch knew he should find Mr. Phibbs and get back to Lilo, but he couldn't resist trying his own experiment.

With some careful pours and shakes, Stitch created a stink bomb that sent everyone scrambling from the room . . . including his froggy friend.

The hallway was filled with students headed toward the cafeteria. How would he ever find Mr. Phibbs in that crowd? Stitch followed all the students as they filed into the cafeteria searching for the little green frog.

Stitch didn't have to worry. Mr. Phibbs hopped right behind him to the cafeteria. Stitch tried to grab him . . . but missed. Mr. Phibbs jumped right onto a tray spilling food everywhere.

"Food fight!"

As the cafeteria erupted into chaos, Stitch spotted Mr. Phibbs jumping out the door.

As the frog hopped from room to room, Stitch followed. But every time he got close, something new caught his eye. He was doing math when he remembered what Nani had said about "best behavior." School was interesting, but the clock was ticking and he needed to get back to class with Mr. Phibbs—and fast!

At last, Stitch found Mr. Phibbs . . .

. . . just as a whistle blew and red rubber balls filled the air. Stitch ducked, jumped, and cartwheeled across the gymnasium . . . and caught Mr. Phibbs. Now he could get back to Lilo's class.

And just in time! It was Lilo's turn to introduce her pet for Pet Day.

"My name is Lilo Pelekai, and this is Stitch," she said. "He's my . . . Stitch!"

"What an . . . unusual pet," said the teacher.

"Yes, ma'am," said Lilo. "That's because
Stitch isn't just a pet. He's my
best friend and part
of my *'ohana*—and
'ohana means
'family.'"

Lilo pulled
Stitch into a
big hug.

Nani met Lilo and Stitch after school.

"Pet Day was great!" Lilo said. "Stitch was on his best behavior."

"Really?" Nani asked. "I mean, really? I think that calls for some ice cream."

Stitch agreed: this was the best Pet Day ever!